The Palace of the Man in Blue

By Idries Shah

Text Copyright © 2023 The Estate of Idries Shah
Illustrations Copyright © 2023 Laetitia Bermejo

ALL RIGHTS RESERVED

No part of this publication may be reproduced or transmitted in any form or by any means, electronic, mechanical, or photographic, by recording, or any information storage or retrieval system or method now known or to be invented or adapted, without prior permission obtained in writing from The Estate of Idries Shah, except by a reviewer quoting brief passages in a review written for inclusion in a journal, magazine, newspaper or broadcast.

Requests for permission to reprint, reproduce, etc. to:
HSLF, 548 Market St., # 39187, San Francisco, CA 94104-5401, USA.

Originally published in *The Dermis Probe,* The Octagon Press 1970

Published by Hoopoe Books,
a division of The Institute for the Study of Human Knowledge,
in collaboration with Kashfi's Children

ISBN: 978-1-959393-62-7

hoopoebooks.com

kashfischildren.org

Visit hoopoebooks.com for a complete list of Hoopoe titles and free downloadable resources for parents and teachers.

Library of Congress Cataloging-in-Publication Data

Names: Shah, Idries, 1924-1996, author. | Bermejo, Laetitia, illustrator.
Title: The palace of the man in blue / by Idries Shah ; illustrated by
   Laetitia Bermejo.
Description: San Francisco, CA : Hoopoe Books, 2024. | Audience: Ages 8-11
   | Audience: Grades 2-3 | Summary: "Four traveling merchants stumble upon
   a magnificent palace. Once inside, they meet a mysterious man dressed in
   blue, and things happen that make them each question their past
   experiences and assumptions."-- Provided by publisher.
Identifiers: LCCN 2023053340 | ISBN 9781959393627 (paperback)
Subjects: CYAC: Folklore. | LCGFT: Folk tales. | Picture books.
Classification: LCC PZ8.1.S47 Pal 2024 | DDC 398.2--dc23/eng/20231220
LC record available at https://lccn.loc.gov/2023053340

The Palace of the Man in Blue

Idries Shah

One day, four merchants stopped to rest at the gates of a magnificent palace.

"Never before have I seen such wealth!" exclaimed one merchant.

"Can those really be gold tiles on the roof?" cried another.

The merchants' gasps of wonder were cut short by the arrival of a finely dressed steward, who invited them into the palace grounds to take refreshments.

Only too delighted to agree, the travelers followed the steward into the courtyard.

Here, they saw a large crowd gathered.

At the center of this crowd was a man dressed in blue.

He appeared to be healing the people assembled.

One by one, the lame threw down their crutches,

and the blind exclaimed that they could see.

"This is the strangest thing I have ever witnessed," said one of the merchants. "I know this man. I have met him hobbling about my hometown with a multitude of ailments of his own. Yet here at his own home he appears to be a healer."

The steward continued his tour, asking the merchants to follow him to the main hall, where they were treated to a splendid meal.

"Now it's my turn to be amazed," said a second merchant.
"I, too, know the man in blue."

"I have seen him imploring people in my town for scraps of food.
Yet now he treats us to a feast fit for a king!"

When the meal was finished, the steward took the merchants to see his master's gardens, which stretched as far as the eye could see.

Every fruit imaginable hung from the orchard's trees.

Every flower was in perfect bloom in the flowerbeds.

"Five hundred gardeners must be employed here!" whispered the third merchant. "Yet their master used to trudge through my neighborhood seeking work for himself."

Minute by minute, the visitors' wonderment increased.

On they went, passing fountains running with crystal-clear water, exotic pets roaming on the lush grass, and entertainers amusing the people walking in the extensive grounds.

"He must be spending more here in a single day than a king does in a year," mused the fourth merchant, astonished. "Yet I have seen him begging for coins on the streets of my town."

The day wore on.

The sun started to cast long shadows across the grounds.

The merchants realized that what they had thought would be a short break in their journey had taken up most of the afternoon.

And, puzzled, they reflected on how they all had previously met the man in blue and that when they had met him, he was eking out a meager existence, heavily reliant on the charity of those around him.

The man in blue summoned his steward and instructed him to show the guests back to their wares.

"I shall rest now," he said, "but be sure to answer any questions these visitors might have. It would be inhospitable of me to leave them perplexed in any way."

Escorting the merchants back to the palace gates,
the steward offered to satisfy their curiosity.

The first merchant said, "My question is: If your master is able to heal people when he is at home, why does he suffer from multiple ailments when he passes through my town?"

The steward smiled but said nothing.

"I'd like to know why he asks for scraps of food in my town when here he has tables groaning with the finest food I have ever seen," said the second merchant.

The steward remained silent.

"What about his gardens?" quizzed the third merchant. "He grows every plant imaginable and employs countless gardeners to tend them, but I have seen him imploring people in my town to give him work, even for a few hours."

The fourth merchant asked, "And why does he beg for money in my town when clearly he can afford to spend a fortune here?"

The steward's expression didn't change; neither did he provide an answer.

"Your master told you to satisfy our curiosity," muttered the first merchant, "yet you say nothing now although you have been perfectly responsive for the whole afternoon."

The steward patted the fine buttons on his waistcoat of woven gold, adjusted his lavish wig, and flicked a little imaginary lint from his sleeve.

"Forgive me," he said. "You have each asked a question, but I have only one answer because your four questions are really all the same."

"My master has given you each a chance to help him by offering him medical aid, or food, or employment, or money."

The merchants shifted nervously.

"Sometimes you and your neighbors have been generous.

And sometimes you and they have not."

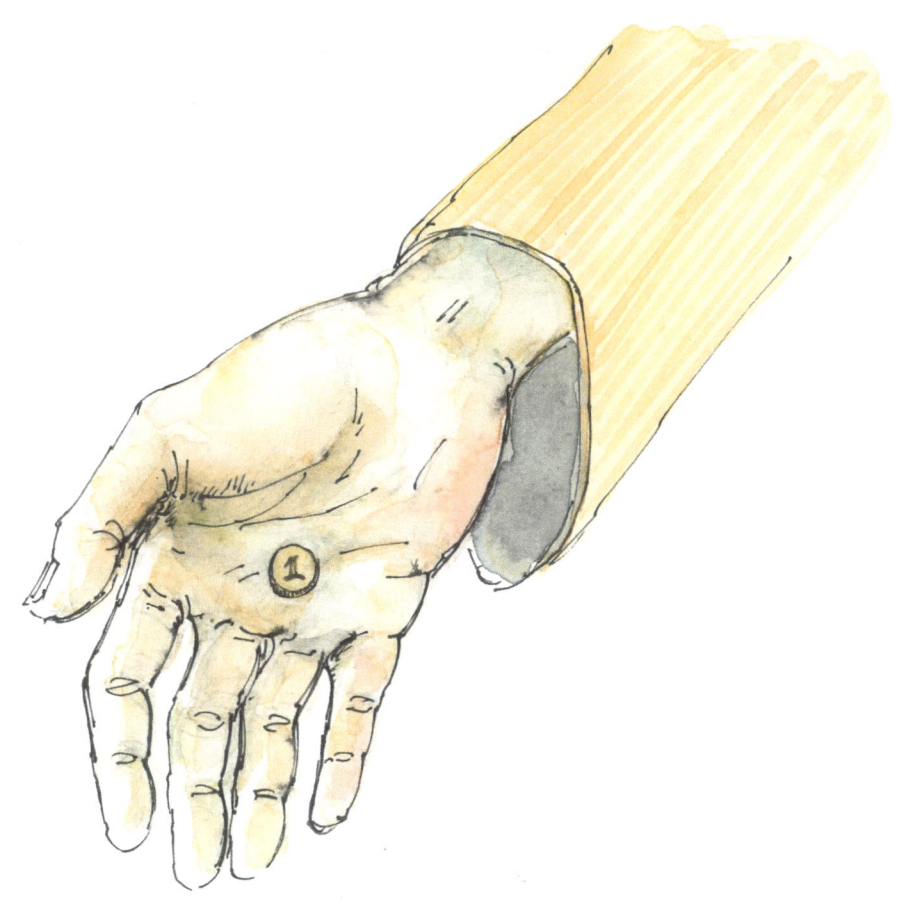

"By giving you each the opportunity to help him, my master has made it possible for you to help yourselves.

When a needy man asks for help and you help him, you help yourself. The way to do good is thus kept open all the time, among all communities, in every possible manner."

And with that, the steward, the gates and the palace of the man in blue melted away.

the End

TEACHING STORIES FOR CHILDREN BY IDRIES SHAH

The Bird's Relative
Oinkink
The Spoiled Boy With the Terribly Dry Throat
Peaches
The King Without a Trade
The Palace of the Man in Blue
The Farmer's Wife
The Lion Who Saw Himself in the Water
The Clever Boy and the Terrible, Dangerous Animal
The Man with Bad Manners
The Silly Chicken
The Man and the Fox
The Old Woman and the Eagle
The Boy Without a Name
Neem the Half-Boy
Fatima the Spinner and the Tent
The Magic Horse

'Our experiences show that while reading Idries Shah stories can help children with reading and writing, the stories can also help them transcend fixed patterns of emotion and behaviour which may be getting in the way of learning and emotional well-being.'
Ezra Hewing, Head of Education at the mental-health charity Suffolk Mind in Suffolk, UK; and Kashfi Khan, teacher at Hounslow Town Primary School in London

Printed in the USA
CPSIA information can be obtained
at www.ICGtesting.com
LVHW072054300524
781675LV00004B/47